ROY G. BIV

IS MAD AT ME

BECAUSE
I LOVE PINK!

**Story by
Nancy Guettier**

Illustrated by Andrew Vera

NEW YORK

ROY G. BIV
IS MAD AT ME
BECAUSE
I LOVE PINK!

ISBN 978-1-61448-671-8 paperback

Morgan James Publishing
The Entrepreneurial Publisher
5 Penn Plaza, 23rd Floor,
New York City, New York 10001
(212) 655-5470 office • (516) 908-4496 fax
www.MorganJamesPublishing.com

In an effort to support local communities, raise awareness and funds, Morgan James Publishing donates a percentage of all book sales for the life of each book to Habitat for Humanity Peninsula and Greater Williamsburg.

Get involved today, visit
www.MorganJamesBuilds.com.

Habitat for Humanity®
Peninsula and
Greater Williamsburg
Building Partner

THIS BOOK IS DEDICATED TO MY DAUGHTER, **GENEVIEVE,** AND ALL GIRLS WHO LOVE PINK!

Learn about the colors by making
friends with **ROY G BIV**.
The color order of the rainbow is
red·**orange**·yellow·**green**·**blue**·**indigo**·**violet**

Genevieve woke up every morning in a pink room tucked in her pink bed with her pink sheets.

She would get dressed every morning in her pink dress.

She'd tie a matching pink bow in her hair.

And of course, she'd wear a pair of cute pink shoes.

She Loves Pink!

One rainy day Genevieve put on her pink polka dot raincoat, matching pink rain boots and of course, a pink umbrella, and went outside to jump in the puddles.

When the rain stopped she sat on the porch and looked up at the sky. That's when she met...

ROY G BIV, and he was mad at her because

She Loves Pink!

Roy said to Genevieve, "There are many colors in the spectrum, I think you'd like them if you met them. There is so much more you could do with another hue or two."

"Who are you," she said, "and what business is it to you?"

"My name is ROY G BIV."

"That's quite a name. How'd you get a name like that?" Genevieve asked.

Roy was proud to say the origins of his name. "It's ROY G BIV. The colors of the rainbow, the spectrum in the sky.
R is for Red
O is for Orange
Y is for Yellow
G is for Green
B is for Blue
I is for Indigo
V is for Violet

What's your name?"

"Genevieve," she replied. "Why are you so mad Roy?"

"I am mad because most people forget the beauty of color and only have one favorite. Let me introduce you to a hue or two..."

"Meet the color Red," he said.
"Red is the color of beautiful big hearts.
It's fiery and passionate and exciting!
The most emotionally intense color.
It is also the color of love. Red mixed
with white is pink, so you should love
RED, don't you think?"

"Indeed it is a stimulating color but I prefer
pink and no other..."

"Well please try Orange**. Orange is a combination of yellow and red. It's a juicy color named after the fruit. Just like orange juice, it gives you energy and stimulates creative thought. It adds a little spice to everything in life. Isn't that nice?"**

"Orange is exciting and warm. I do love how it makes me think, but Roy, I still prefer PINK!"

"Yellow is a happy color. Yellow is bright, cheery and warm. Yellow is an attention-getter. It's a color that makes you feel happiness and joy."

"While yellow is catchy and bright, I still like pink and I don't want to fight."

"How about Green? Green symbolizes nature and it's in the trees and the growing grass. It is how we want to live. Green is calm and refreshing.

"Green does make a pretty scene, but pink is how I dream."

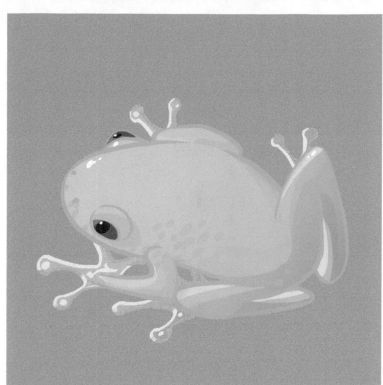

"Well how about Blue? It's like the sky above and the beautiful blue birds that fly. Blue is calm and serene like the ocean scene."

"Blue is soothing I must say, but I still like pink anyway."

"Indigo is a very deep purple, and it's a color of honor, valor and purpose. Indigo is like the darkest night sky."

"It's a mysterious color I can see, but pink still pleases me."

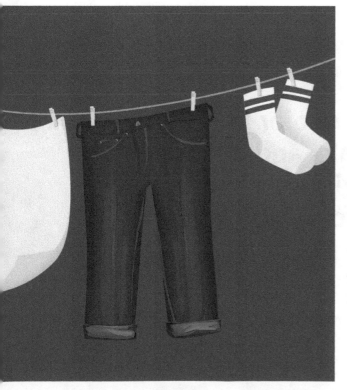

"Violet is the last color in my spectrum. It's a softer purple, and it's pretty on flowers and ribbons and bows. It's a beautiful color, you know."

"Violet is lovely I agree," she said. "But Pink is the only color for me."

"Well the clouds are clearing and I must go. The colors will all come together to say goodbye, and they hope one day you'll give them a try."

As the clouds parted, the rainbow brushed the sky and it was magnificent! All the flowers perked up and showed their colors. Reds and blues and vibrant greens. It was a magical scene.

Genevieve cried. "I see now Roy. Thank you for showing me the colors of the world."

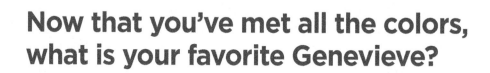

**Now that you've met all the colors,
what is your favorite Genevieve?**

With a big smile Genevieve said,
"I still love pink as you know.
But now I must say my favorite color
is RAINBOW!"

The end.

CPSIA information can be obtained
at www.ICGtesting.com
Printed in the USA
BVHW091616160919
558546BV00022BA/2000